The Velveteen Rabbit
or How Toys Become Real

Margery Williams

Illustrated by Loretta Krupinski

Hyperion Books for Children
New York

Illustrations © 1997 by Loretta Krupinksi.

Printed in the United States of America.

First Edition

1 3 5 7 9 10 8 6 4 2

The artwork for each picture is prepared
using gouache and colored pencils.
This book is set in 16/24 Centaur.

Library of Congress Cataloging-in-Publication Data
Bianco, Margery Williams, 1880-1944.
The velveteen rabbit, or, how toys become real / Margery Williams;
abridged and illustrated by Loretta Krupinski. — 1st ed.
p.   cm.
Summary: By the time the velveteen rabbit is dirty, worn out, and
about to be burned, he has almost given up hope of ever finding the
magic called Real.
ISBN 0-7868-0319-3 (trade)
[1. Toys—Fiction.]   I. Krupinski, Loretta, ill.   II. Title.
PZ7.B4713Ve   1996b
[E]—dc20   96-31209

The Velveteen Rabbit

here was once a velveteen rabbit, and in the beginning he was really splendid. He was fat and bunchy, as a rabbit should be; his coat was spotted brown and white, he had real thread whiskers, and his ears were lined with pink sateen. On Christmas morning, when he sat wedged in the top of the Boy's stocking, with a sprig of holly between his paws, the effect was charming.

There were other things in the stocking, nuts and oranges and a toy engine, and chocolate almonds and a clockwork mouse, but the Rabbit was quite the best of all. For at least two hours the Boy loved him, and then Aunts and Uncles came to dinner, and there was a great rustling of parcels, and in the excitement of looking at all the new presents the Velveteen Rabbit was forgotten.

or a long time he lived in the toy cupboard or on the nursery floor, and no one thought very much about him. He was naturally shy, and being only made of velveteen, some of the more expensive toys quite naturally snubbed him. The only person who was kind to him at all was the Skin Horse.

The Skin Horse had lived longer in the nursery than any of the others. He was so old that his coat was bald in patches and showed the seams underneath. He was wise, for he had seen a long succession of mechanical toys arrive to boast and swagger, and by and by break their mainsprings and pass away, and he knew that they were only toys, and would never turn into anything else. For nursery magic is very strange and wonderful, and only those playthings that are old and wise and experienced like the Skin Horse understand all about it.

"hat is REAL?" asked the Rabbit one day.

"Real isn't how you are made," said the Skin Horse. "It's a thing that happens to you. When a child loves you for a long, long time, not just to play with, but REALLY loves you, then you become Real."

"Does it hurt?" asked the Rabbit.

"Sometimes," said the Skin Horse, for he was always truthful. "When you are Real you don't mind being hurt."

"Does it happen all at once, or bit by bit?"

"It doesn't happen all at once," said the Skin Horse. "You become. It takes a long time. That's why it doesn't often happen to people who break easily, or have sharp edges, or who have to be carefully kept. Generally, by the time you are Real, most of your hair has been loved off, and your eyes drop out, and you get loose in the joints and very shabby. But these things don't matter at all, because once you are Real you can't be ugly, except to people who don't understand."

"I suppose you are Real?" said the Rabbit.

"The Boy's Uncle made me Real. That was a great many years ago."

he Rabbit sighed. He thought it would be a long time before this magic called Real happened to him. He longed to become Real, to know what it felt like.

There was one person called Nana who ruled the nursery. Sometimes she took no notice of the playthings lying about, and sometimes, for no reason whatever, she went swooping about like a great wind and hustled them away in cupboards. She called this "tidying up," and the playthings all hated it.

One evening, when the Boy was going to bed, he couldn't find the china dog that always slept with him. Nana was in a hurry, so she simply looked about her, and seeing that the toy cupboard door stood open, she made a swoop.

"Here," she said, "take your old Bunny! He'll do to sleep with you!" And she dragged the Rabbit out by one ear, and put him into the Boy's arms.

hat night, and for many nights after, the Velveteen Rabbit slept in the Boy's bed. At first he found it rather uncomfortable, for the Boy hugged him very tight, and sometimes he pushed him so far under the pillow that the Rabbit could scarcely breathe. But very soon he grew to like it, for the Boy used to talk to him, and made nice tunnels for him under the bedclothes that he said were like the burrows the real rabbits lived in. And when the Boy dropped off to sleep, the Rabbit would snuggle down close under his little warm chin and dream, with the Boy's hands clasped close round him all night long.

And so time went on, and the little Rabbit was very happy—so happy that he never noticed how his beautiful velveteen fur was getting shabbier and shabbier, and his tail was coming unsewn, and all the pink had rubbed off his nose where the Boy had kissed him.

pring came, and they had long days in the garden, for wherever the Boy went the Rabbit went too. He had rides in the wheelbarrow, and picnics on the grass, and lovely fairy huts built for him under the raspberry canes.

Once, the Rabbit was left out on the lawn until long after dusk, and Nana had to come and look for him because the Boy couldn't go to sleep unless he was there. He was wet through with dew and Nana grumbled as she rubbed him off with a corner of her apron. "Fancy all this fuss for a toy!" she said.

The Boy sat up in his bed and stretched out his hands. "Give me my Bunny!" he said. "You mustn't say that. He isn't a toy. He's REAL!"

The Rabbit knew that what the Skin Horse had said was true at last. The magic had happened to him, and he was a toy no longer. He was Real.

That night he was almost too happy to sleep, and so much love stirred in his little sawdust heart that it almost burst. And into his boot-button eyes there came a look of wisdom and beauty, so that even Nana noticed it the next morning and said, "I declare if that old Bunny hasn't got quite a knowing expression!"

ear the house where they lived there was a wood, and in the long June evenings the Boy liked to go there after tea to play. He took the Velveteen Rabbit with him, and made the Rabbit a little nest somewhere among the bracken. One evening, while the Rabbit was lying there alone, he saw two strange beings creep out of the tall bracken near him.

They were rabbits like himself, but quite furry and brand-new. They must have been very well made, for their seams didn't show at all, and they changed shape in a queer way when they moved; one minute they were long and thin and the next minute fat and bunchy, instead of always staying the same like he did. Their feet padded softly on the ground, and they crept quite close to him, twitching their noses, while the Rabbit stared hard to see which side the clockwork stuck out, for he knew that people who jump generally have something to wind them up. But he couldn't see it. They were evidently a new kind of rabbit altogether.

They stared at him, and the little Rabbit stared back. And all the time their noses twitched.

hy don't you get up and play with us?" one of them asked.

"I don't feel like it," said the Rabbit.

"Can you hop on your hind legs?" asked the furry rabbit.

That was a dreadful question, for the Velveteen Rabbit had no hind legs at all!

"I don't want to!" he said again.

But wild rabbits have very sharp eyes. And this one stretched out his neck and looked.

"He hasn't got any hind legs!" he called out. "Fancy a rabbit without any hind legs!" And he began to laugh.

Then the strange rabbit came quite close. He wrinkled his nose suddenly and flattened his ears and jumped backward. "He doesn't smell right!" he exclaimed. "He isn't a rabbit at all! He isn't real!"

"I am Real!" said the little Rabbit. "The Boy said so!" Just then there was a sound of footsteps, and the two strange rabbits disappeared.

"Come back and play with me!" called the Rabbit. "I *know* I am Real!"

But there was no answer. The Velveteen Rabbit was all alone.

eeks passed, and the little Rabbit grew very old and shabby, but the Boy loved him just as much. He loved him so hard that he loved almost all his whiskers off, and the pink lining of his ears turned grey, and his spots faded. To the Boy he was always beautiful, and that was all that the little Rabbit cared about.

And then, one day, the Boy was ill.

His face grew very flushed, and he talked in his sleep, and his little body was so hot that it burned the Rabbit when he held him close. Strange people came and went in the nursery, and a light burned all night, and through it all the little Velveteen Rabbit lay there, hidden from sight under the bedclothes, and he never stirred, for he was afraid that if they found him someone might take him away, and he knew that the Boy needed him.

It was a long weary time, for the Boy was too ill to play. But the Rabbit snuggled down patiently, and looked forward to the time when the Boy should be well again.

resently the fever turned, and the Boy got better. It was a bright, sunny morning, and the windows stood wide open. They had carried the Boy outside, wrapped in a shawl, and the little Rabbit lay tangled up among the bedclothes, thinking.

The Boy was going to the seaside tomorrow. Everything was arranged, and now it only remained to carry out the doctor's orders. They talked about it all, while the little Rabbit lay under the bedclothes, with just his head peeping out, and listened. The room was to be disinfected, and all the books and toys that the Boy had played with in bed must be burnt.

Just then Nana caught sight of him.

"How about this old Bunny?" she asked.

"*That?*" said the doctor. "Why, it's a mass of scarlet fever germs!—Burn it at once. What? Nonsense! Get him a new one. He mustn't have that anymore!"

nd so the little Rabbit was put into a sack with the old picture books and a lot of rubbish, and carried out to the end of the garden behind the fowl-house. That was a fine place to make a bonfire, only the gardener was too busy just then to attend to it.

That night the Boy slept in a different bedroom, and he had a new bunny to sleep with him. It was a splendid bunny, all white plush with real glass eyes, but the boy was too excited to care very much about it. For tomorrow he was going to the seaside, and that in itself was such a wonderful thing that he could think of nothing else.

And while the Boy was asleep, dreaming of the seaside, the little Rabbit lay among the old picture books in the corner behind the fowl-house, and he felt very lonely. He thought of those long sunlit hours in the garden—how happy they were—and a great sadness came over him. He thought of the Skin Horse, so wise and gentle, and all that he had told him. Of what use was it to be loved and become Real if it all ended like this? And a tear, a real tear, trickled down his little shabby velvet nose and fell to the ground.

nd then a strange thing happened. For where the tear had fallen a flower grew out of the ground, a mysterious flower, not at all like any that grew in the garden. It was so beautiful that the little Rabbit forgot to cry, and just lay there watching it. And presently the blossom opened, and out of it there stepped a fairy.

She was quite the loveliest fairy in the whole world. There were flowers round her neck and in her hair, and her face was like the most perfect flower of all. And she came close to the little Rabbit and kissed him on his velveteen nose that was all damp from crying.

"I am the nursery magic Fairy," she said. "I take care of all the playthings that the children have loved. When they are old and worn out and the children don't need them anymore, then I come and take them away with me and turn them into Real."

"Wasn't I Real before?" asked the little Rabbit.

"You were real to the Boy," the Fairy said, "because he loved you. Now you shall be Real to everyone."

Together they went into the wood.

n an open glade in the woods, the wild rabbits danced with their shadows on the velvet grass, but when they saw the Fairy they all stopped dancing and stood round in a ring to stare at her.

"I've brought you a new playfellow," the Fairy said. And she kissed the little Rabbit again and put him down on the grass.

"Run and play, little Rabbit!" she said.

But the little Rabbit sat quite still. For when he saw all the wild rabbits dancing around him he suddenly remembered about his hind legs. He did not know that when the Fairy kissed him that last time she had changed him altogether. And he might have sat there a long time, too shy to move, if just then something hadn't tickled his nose, and before he thought what he was doing he lifted his hind toe to scratch it.

And he found that he actually had hind legs! Instead of dingy velveteen he had brown fur, soft and shiny, and his whiskers were so long that they brushed the grass. He gave one leap and the joy of using those hind legs was so great that he went springing about the turf on them, jumping sideways and whirling round as the others did.

He was a Real Rabbit at last.

utumn passed and Winter, and in the Spring, when the days grew warm and sunny, the Boy went out to play in the wood behind the house. And while he was playing, two rabbits crept out from the bracken and peeped at him. One of them was brown all over, but the other had strange markings under his fur, as though long ago he had been spotted, and the spots still showed through. And about his little soft nose and his round black eyes there was something familiar, so that the Boy thought to himself: "Why, he looks just like my old Bunny that was lost when I had scarlet fever!"

But he never knew that it really was his own Bunny, come back to look at the child who had first helped him to be Real.